Holly
the Christmas Fairy

For Holly Sarah Williams,
my beautiful niece

Special thanks to
Narinder Dhami

www.rainbowmagic.co.uk

ORCHARD BOOKS
96 Leonard Street, London EC2A 4XD
Orchard Books Australia
32/45-51 Huntley Street, Alexandria, NSW 2015
A Paperback Original
First published in Great Britain in 2004
Text © Working Partners Limited 2004
Created by Working Partners Limited, London W6 0QT
Illustrations © Georgie Ripper 2004
The right of Georgie Ripper to be identified as the illustrator
of this work has been asserted by her in accordance
with the Copyright, Designs and Patents Act, 1988.
A CIP catalogue record for this book is available
from the British Library.
ISBN 1 84362 661 6
7 9 10 8
Printed in Great Britain

Holly
the Christmas Fairy

by Daisy Meadows
illustrated by Georgie Ripper

ORCHARD BOOKS

The Fairyland Palace

Hillfields Farm

Christmas Trees

HILLFIELDS FARM

Tippington Town

Santa's Missing Sleigh

Christmas plans may go awry,
If I can make these reindeer fly.
Santa,s gifts for girls and boys
Shall all become my sweets and toys!

Magic reindeer listen well,
As now I bind you with this spell.
Heed my bidding, fly this sleigh
Through starry skies and far away.

Contents

A Magical Mistake   9

Christmas Chaos   21

Buttons on the Loose!   37

Grumpy Goblins   47

Holly's Magic Trick   53

A Magical Mistake

"Only three days to go!" Rachel
Walker sighed happily. She was pinning
Christmas cards onto long pieces of
red ribbon, ready to hang on the
living-room wall. "I love Christmas!
Don't you, Kirsty?"

Kirsty Tate, Rachel's best friend,
nodded. "Of course I do," she replied,

handing Rachel another pile of cards. "It's a magical time, isn't it?"

Rachel and Kirsty laughed, and touched the golden lockets they both wore around their necks.

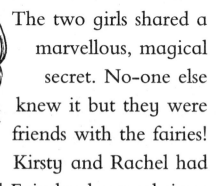

The two girls shared a marvellous, magical secret. No-one else knew it but they were friends with the fairies! Kirsty and Rachel had visited Fairyland several times when their help had been needed. The first time, they had rescued the Rainbow Fairies after they were banished by Jack Frost's nasty spell. Then Jack Frost and his goblin servants had stolen the magic tail feathers from Doodle, the cockerel in

charge of fairy weather. The girls had
helped the Weather Fairies to get
Doodle's feathers back.

In return, the Fairy King and Queen
had given gold lockets to Rachel and
Kirsty. The lockets were full of magic
fairy dust which the girls could use to
take them to Fairyland if ever they
needed help from the fairies.

"Thanks for asking me
to stay," said Kirsty,
cutting another piece
of ribbon. "Mum says
she and Dad will collect
me on Christmas Eve."

"We might get some snow before
then!" Rachel smiled. "The weather's
getting much colder. I wonder what
Christmas is like in Fairyland…"

At that moment, the door opened and
Mrs Walker came in. She was followed
by Buttons, Rachel's friendly, shaggy
dog. He was white with grey patches
and a long, furry tail.

"Oh, girls, that looks lovely!" Rachel's
mum exclaimed when she saw the cards
hanging on the walls. "We'll go over
to Lakeland Farm and choose a
Christmas tree this evening."

"Hurrah!" said Rachel. "Can Kirsty and I decorate it?"

"We were hoping you would!" her mother laughed. "You'd better get the decorations out of the garage after lunch."

"Buttons seems to love Christmas too," Kirsty said smiling. The dog was sniffing around the cards and ribbons.

"He does," Rachel replied. "Every year I buy him some doggie treats and wrap them up. And every year he finds them and eats them before Christmas!"

Buttons wagged his tail. Then he grabbed the end of a ribbon in his mouth, and ran off, trailing red ribbon behind him.

"Buttons, no!" Rachel yelled, and she and Kirsty ran after him to get the ribbon back. When the girls had finished hanging the Christmas cards, it was time for a delicious lunch of hot soup. Then Rachel took Kirsty out to the garage to fetch the decorations.

"It's getting colder," Kirsty said, shivering. "Maybe it will snow."

"I hope so," Rachel replied. She switched the garage light on. "The decorations are up there." She pointed at a shelf above the workbench. "I'll stand on the stepladder and hand the boxes down to you."

"OK," Kirsty agreed.

Rachel climbed up the ladder, and began to lift the boxes down. They were full of silver stars, shiny tinsel and glittering baubles in pink, purple and silver.

"I hope you've got a fairy for the top of the tree!" Kirsty joked, as Rachel handed her a box.

"No, we don't!" Rachel laughed. "We've always had a silver star, but it's getting quite old and tatty now. Be careful, Kirsty," she went on, lifting another box from the shelf. "This one's got all sorts of things sticking out of it. Oh!" Rachel gasped with surprise.

The gold locket around her neck had caught on a little sparkling wreath made of twigs. The locket burst open, scattering fairy dust all over both girls.

"Oh, no!" Rachel cried, scrambling down from the ladder.

"What shall we do?" Kirsty began.

But they didn't have time to do anything. Suddenly, both girls were caught up in a swirling cloud of fairy dust that swept them off their feet. The sparkles whirled around them, glittering in the pale winter light.

"Kirsty, we're shrinking!" Rachel cried. "I think we're on our way to Fairyland!"

Christmas Chaos

The girls weren't scared because this had happened to them before. But, as they whirled through the clouds towards Fairyland, Rachel felt a bit embarrassed. She hadn't meant to use her magic fairy dust at all – it was an accident!

"Don't worry," called Kirsty, seeing the look on Rachel's face. "It'll be lovely to see our fairy friends again."

Soon the girls spotted the red and white toadstool houses of Fairyland below them, and then the silver palace with its four pink turrets. As the girls drifted closer to the palace, they could see a crowd of fairies waving at them. There was King Oberon and Queen Titania, with the Rainbow Fairies and

all the Weather Fairies, too.
Even Doodle, the fairy
cockerel, had come
to greet them.
"Hello!"
called Ruby
and Saffron.
"It's wonderful
to see you!"
cried Pearl
and Storm.
As the girls
landed on the
ground, the fairies
crowded around them.
Rachel quickly tried to
explain. "I'm sorry,"
she gasped. "We didn't mean
to come. It was an accident."

The Queen smiled. "No, it wasn't an accident!" she said in her silvery voice. "Our magic made your locket open. I'm afraid we need your help again, girls!"

The two friends turned to stare at each other in surprise, their eyes wide.

"Not Jack Frost again?" Kirsty asked.
"Hasn't he been banished to the end of the rainbow?" Rachel added.

"We'll tell you all about it," replied
the Queen. "But first…"
She waved her wand
at Rachel's locket. It
filled with fairy dust
again, and closed,
all on its own.
   "Now," the King
said, turning to the fairies.
"Where is Holly, the Christmas Fairy?"
   Kirsty and Rachel watched eagerly as
Holly came forward. They had never
met the Christmas Fairy before. She had
long dark hair, and she wore a little red
dress, exactly the same colour as a holly
berry. The dress had a hood with furry
white trim, and she wore tiny red boots.
But although she was the Christmas
Fairy, Holly looked rather sad.

"Holly is in charge of putting the sparkle into Christmas," Queen Titania explained.

"That's right," Holly sighed. "I organise Santa's elves, and I teach the reindeer to fly. It's my job to make sure that Christmas is as sparkly and happy as possible."

"But this year Jack Frost is causing trouble," the King told them. "We let him come back from the end of the rainbow because he said he was sorry and he promised to behave."

"And we agreed that he could help Doodle with the wintry weather," said Queen Titania.

"So what happened?" Rachel asked.

"Well, Jack Frost sent a letter to Father Christmas asking for presents," the King went on. "But he got a letter back saying he'd been so naughty, he wouldn't be getting anything this year!"

"We'll show you what Jack Frost did next," said the Queen. She waved her wand over a small pool of blue water which lay amongst the flowers. The water bubbled and fizzed, and then became smooth as glass.

Pictures began to appear on the surface. Kirsty and Rachel saw a large log cabin at night time. It was surrounded by deep snow, and icicles hung from the wooden roof. Inside, the cabin was full of toys. There were dolls, jigsaws, bikes, games, puzzles and

books, all lying around in huge heaps.
Kirsty and Rachel had never seen so
many toys.

"Oh!" Kirsty gasped, her hand flying
to her mouth. "Rachel, look!"

In the corner of the cabin stood a
beautiful wooden rocking-horse.
Someone was painting gold patterns
onto the rockers. He was all dressed in
red and white, and he had a jolly face
with a long white beard.

"It's Father Christmas!" Rachel cried
happily.

Then the picture changed to show the outside of the cabin again. There the girls could see Santa's sleigh. It was silver and white, and sparkled with magic. Eight reindeer were harnessed to the sleigh, all ready to go. They were waiting patiently, shaking their antlers every so often.

Lots of little elves wearing bright green tunics scurried around the sleigh, filling it with presents. The bells on the tips of their hats tinkled merrily as they rushed here and there with armfuls of parcels.

Kirsty and Rachel were so delighted,
they almost forgot why they were
watching. But then, just as the sleigh
was full to bursting with presents, the
thin, spiky figure of Jack Frost
appeared.

As Kirsty and Rachel
watched, Jack Frost
peeped out from behind
the log cabin. When
there were no elves
near the sleigh, he ran
over to it and jumped
in. Grabbing the reins,
he shouted a spell to
make the reindeer obey
him. And the next moment, the
sleigh lifted off the ground and zoomed
away into the starry night sky.

As soon as the elves saw what was
happening, they gave
chase, but the
magic sleigh was
much too fast for
them to catch.

"Oh, how could he?" Kirsty said
crossly. "He's stolen Santa's sleigh!"

"So now you see why we need your
help," said Queen Titania, as the
pictures faded away. "Holly must find
Santa's sleigh and return it before
Christmas Eve, or Christmas will be
ruined for all the children around the
world!"

"We think Jack Frost has taken the
sleigh to your world," Holly added. "He
loves parties, so he won't want to miss
Christmas. Will you help me?"

"Of course we will," Rachel and Kirsty replied together.

Holly smiled. "Thank you!" she cried, giving both girls a hug.

"Where should we start looking?" asked Rachel.

"As always, the magic will come to you," Titania said with a smile. "You'll know when you are on the right track. And Holly will help. But there is one more thing you need to know..." The Queen waved her wand over the pool once more, and the girls watched as an image of three presents appeared.

They were wrapped in beautiful golden paper, and tied with big bows that glittered in all the colours of the rainbow.

"These three presents were on the sleigh when Jack Frost took it and they are very special," the Queen explained. "So please try to find them."

"We'll do our best," said Kirsty, and Rachel nodded.

The King stepped forward, holding a soft golden bag. "This can help you to defeat Jack Frost," he said, opening the bag and showing the girls a sparkling fairy crown. "It has powerful magic. If

Jack Frost puts it on, he
will immediately be
brought here to
appear before Queen
Titania and me."

Kirsty took the bag and
put the strap safely over her shoulder.

"Good luck, Rachel and Kirsty!"
called the Queen. She raised her wand
and sent another shower of fairy dust
whirling and swirling around the girls.
Rachel and Kirsty were lifted off their
feet to begin the journey home.

Buttons on the Loose!

"We're back!" Rachel said, as the sparkling clouds of fairy dust cleared. They were in the Walkers' garage again.

"And we're back to normal size," Kirsty added, brushing a speck of fairy dust from her jeans. "Poor Holly. I hope we can help."

"We'll find mean old Jack Frost!" said Rachel. "But we'd better take these decorations inside now. Mum will be wondering where we've been."

Kirsty popped the tiny golden bag into her pocket for safe-keeping. Then she helped Rachel carry the boxes into the house. There they started looking through the decorations.

"I see what you mean
about the star," Kirsty
said, holding up a
large but tattered
silver star.

"Maybe Mum will
let me buy something
new for the top of the
tree," replied Rachel. "I'd love to have
a fairy this year!"

The girls spent the afternoon sorting
out the decorations. Rachel's dad
arrived home from work at six o'clock,
and then they all went to Lakeland
Farm to choose the Christmas tree.

"It looks like everyone's had the same
idea!" remarked Rachel's mum, as the
car drew up outside the farm. Lots of
people were looking at Christmas trees.

There seemed to be hundreds of them in all shapes and sizes.

"At least there are plenty of trees!" Kirsty laughed.

"And we'll find the perfect one," said Rachel, climbing out of the car.

The two girls hurried over to the farmyard, while Mr and Mrs Walker followed with Buttons. The evening was cold and clear, and stars glittered in the dark sky.

"Don't choose one that's too big," called Mrs Walker. "We'll never get it through the front door."

Rachel and Kirsty wandered up and down the rows of trees. But they couldn't seem to find one which was just right. They were either too big, too small, too bushy or too thin.

Then Rachel's eye was caught by one tree just ahead of her. The needles were so green and shiny, they almost seemed to glow in the frosty air. "That tree looks perfect," she said to herself, as she went over to it. "It's not too big and it's not too small."

Suddenly, Rachel spotted a bright red glow, right in the middle of the tree. Then a tiny face peeped out at her.

"It's me!" Holly cried, waving her wand and sending little sparkly red holly berries bouncing over the tree.

Rachel laughed. "Kirsty, over here!" she called.

Kirsty rushed over. "What are you doing here, Holly?" she asked. "Is Jack Frost close by?"

But before Holly could answer, there
was a shout from Mrs Walker, and
Buttons dashed past the girls, his lead
trailing along behind him. He was
barking loudly.

"Stop him, girls!" puffed Mrs Walker.
"I don't know what's the matter with
him. He pulled the lead right out of my
hand."

"We'll catch him, Mum," Rachel
called. "You look after our tree."

Holly hopped inside Kirsty's pocket,
and then the girls ran after the excited
dog. Buttons had left the farmyard, and
was racing towards an oak tree.

Suddenly, Kirsty saw a shadow dodge
out from behind the tree, and head for
an old barn. Although it
was dark, she could
just about make out
a sharp, pointed
nose and big feet.

"Oh!" she gasped,
"I think Buttons is
chasing one of Jack
Frost's goblins!"

"I knew they were
round here somewhere!"
Holly cried. "Quick! After him!"

Buttons was standing outside
the barn, sniffing at the door.

"The goblin must be inside," Rachel
whispered, grabbing the dog's lead.
Quickly she hooked it over a nail

44

sticking out of the barn wall,
and gave him a pat.
"Wait here quietly,
Buttons," she whispered.
"We won't be long."

"Let's look inside," Kirsty
said. She edged the barn door
open and they all peeped in. A cold
blast of icy air swirled around them.
The girls and Holly could see across the
barn to the large doors at the opposite
end. Those doors were wide open, and
a sparkling trail led out of the barn and
right up into the sky. At the far end of
the trail, they could make out a
glittering silver shape travelling very
fast. It was Santa's missing sleigh!

"Jack Frost was here," Kirsty said, looking disappointed. "We've just missed him."

"That's why it's so cold," Holly agreed with a shiver.

The barn was full of bales of straw, and looking around, Rachel noticed that there was wrapping paper scattered all over them. "Jack Frost has been opening Santa's presents!" she said crossly. "Isn't he mean?"

"Ssh!" Holly whispered. "Goblins!"

Two goblins had just rolled out from behind one of the straw bales near the open doors. They were fighting and yelling at each other.

"It's mine!" shouted one with a wart on his nose.

"No, it's mine!" yelled the other.

"Look," Rachel said. She pointed at the present the goblins were arguing over. "It's one of the three special presents the Queen asked us to look for!"

"We must get that back," said Holly.

"The other two presents must still be on the sleigh," Kirsty added. "I don't see any more of that special gold wrapping paper anywhere about."

The goblins were still fighting, rolling around on the dusty floor of the barn.

"Give it to me!" yelled the warty one. "There might be Christmas cake inside, or brandy snaps, or scrummy mince pies, or—"

"Mince pies!" The other goblin cried, licking his lips. "I'm going to eat them all!"

"What are we going to do?" Rachel whispered. "How are we going to get the present back?"

Kirsty frowned. "I've got an idea," she said. "That goblin seems to like mince pies. Holly, could you magic up the smell of them?"

Holly's eyes twinkled. "Of course," she replied.

"We'll tell the goblins there's a big plate of mince pies in the hayloft," Kirsty went on. "They're so greedy, they're bound to go and look. And they can't climb the ladder and hang on to the parcel. We'll be able to grab it!"

Rachel and Holly beamed at her.

"Great idea!" said Holly. "One magic

smell of hot mince pies coming up!"
And she flew towards the goblins.

Holly's Magic Trick

Rachel and Kirsty watched anxiously as Holly fluttered over the goblins' heads. They were so busy fighting, they didn't notice her.

Holly waved her wand in the air, and a few seconds later the smell of freshly-baked mince pies began to waft around the barn. Even Rachel and Kirsty who were standing outside could smell it.

The goblins stopped fighting. They lifted their big noses into the air and sniffed hard.

"Fresh mince pies!" Holly called, and she pointed at the ladder to the hayloft. "Up in the hayloft. Help yourselves."

"Mince pies! Yum!" shouted one of the goblins. He shoved the present at the other one, and dashed for the ladder.

But the other goblin didn't want to be left behind. He raced over to the ladder too, hot on his friend's heels. As soon as he realised that he couldn't

climb up to the hayloft with the present
in his arms, he threw it down on a pile
of straw.

Rachel and Kirsty
laughed to
themselves, as
they watched
the goblins
scrambling up
the ladder and
trying to shove
each other out
of the way.
When they
had reached
the top, the girls
dashed into the
barn and Kirsty
picked up the parcel.

Suddenly there was a shout from above. "There aren't any mince pies here! We've been tricked!"

One of the goblins peered down into the barn. "Where's that tricksy little Christmas fairy," he yelled.

"Quick!" gasped Holly, "Let's get out of here!"

The girls and Holly dashed for the door as the goblins tumbled down the ladder. "After them!" the first goblin shouted.

Outside the barn Rachel fumbled to
free Buttons' lead from
the nail. The goblins
appeared in the
doorway and ran
towards her. But
Buttons began to bark
loudly as soon as he saw
them. The goblins looked wary.

"You get the present back!" the first
goblin yelled, nudging the other.

"No, you get it!" his friend shouted.

Still barking, Buttons began pulling
Rachel towards them. Immediately, the
two terrified goblins shot back into the
barn and shut the door.

"Good dog!" said Rachel, patting
Buttons to calm him down. Meanwhile,
Kirsty showed the present to Holly.

"Hurrah! We've found one special present," Holly beamed. "I'll get this back to Fairyland right away." She waved her wand over the gift and in a magic cloud of sparkling red holly berries, the present disappeared back to fairyland.

"We'll see you again soon," Rachel called, as Holly fluttered up into the sky.

"I'll be back as soon as I find out where Jack Frost is now!" Holly promised.

Rachel and Kirsty hurried back to the farmyard to find Mr and Mrs Walker. They had bought the tree Rachel had chosen, and were tying it to the roof of the car.

"Now, I think it's time we all went home and had some mince pies and hot chocolate," said Rachel's mum, as they climbed into the car.

Rachel and Kirsty grinned at each other.

"Mince pies would be lovely, Mum," said Rachel, trying not to laugh.

"I think Buttons deserves a mince pie too," Kirsty whispered. "After all, he was the one who led us to the goblins and the first present."

"Woof!" Buttons agreed.

"Yes, and our fairy adventures aren't over yet," Rachel said, her eyes shining. "We'll save the sleigh and this is going to be the best Christmas ever!"

A Narrow
Escape

Contents

Christmas Shopping   65

A Chilling Suspicion   75

Not the Real Santa!   83

The Chase is on . . .   95

The Great Escape   103

Christmas Shopping

"Two days till Christmas!" Rachel said the next morning, as she stood in front of the bedroom mirror, brushing her hair. The girls were getting ready to go Christmas shopping with Rachel's mum. "Isn't it exciting, Kirsty?"

Kirsty nodded. "I can't wait!" she said. "But I don't want it to arrive too soon.

We have to find Jack Frost and Santa's sleigh first."

"I know," Rachel agreed. "Once we've helped our fairy friends, then we can really start to enjoy Christmas."

"I need to buy a present for my mum," Kirsty went on. "Have you got many presents left to buy?"

Rachel shook her head. "Only one," she replied. "But the shopping centre has fantastic Christmas displays, so it's fun to look around even if you haven't got much shopping to do."

"Girls, are you ready yet?" Mrs Walker called up the stairs.

"Coming, Mum," Rachel yelled back.

The girls clattered downstairs, laughing and chatting. Mrs Walker was waiting for them in the hall. "Don't forget your scarves and gloves," she said, picking up her car keys. "It's absolutely freezing today, and the shopping centre car park is outside." She opened the front door, and went to get the car from the garage.

Rachel shivered as a blast of cold air swept through the open door, and rustled through the tinsel on the Christmas tree. "Brr!" she gasped, grabbing her coat. "Mum's right. It is cold today."

"Doesn't the tree look fantastic?" said Kirsty admiringly, pulling on her gloves. The Walkers had a large entrance hall

and they had put the tree in a corner near the stairs. Rachel and Kirsty had decorated it beautifully, and now it glittered and gleamed with baubles, tinsel and toys.

"It's the nicest one we've ever had," Rachel agreed. "But I'll switch the lights off now we're going out."

Kirsty watched as Rachel switched off the Christmas tree lights, and then she noticed that something was different about the tree. Instead of the tired and tattered silver star which she had carefully placed on the top, there now sat a beautiful, sparkly fairy! As Kirsty stared in surprise, she realised that it was a real fairy. Holly was perched at the top of the tree, glowing brightly in her berry-red dress, and waving at Kirsty.

"Holly!" Kirsty laughed. "What are you doing up there?"

"I thought your tree was missing a fairy!" Holly grinned.

Rachel looked up to see Holly fly down from the tree and land on Kirsty's shoulder. "Hello, Rachel," sang Holly in her pretty, tinkly voice. "I have a feeling something magical is going to happen today, so can I come to the shops with you?"

"Of course," Rachel replied, happily. "But you'll have to hide from my mum!"

"No problem," Holly winked at the girls, and snuggled down inside Kirsty's coat pocket, folding her wings away neatly. She popped out a second later to say "Don't forget the magic crown!"

"It's in my pocket," Rachel assured her.

Then they heard Rachel's mum toot the car horn.

"Maybe something magical is going to happen!" Rachel whispered to Kirsty, as they rushed outside. "Maybe today we'll get Santa's sleigh and the two special presents back."

"I hope so!" Kirsty agreed with a smile.

A Chilling Suspicion

Although it was still early in the morning, the shopping centre was already busy when they arrived. Mrs Walker had to queue to get into the car park, and it took them quite a while to find an empty space.

"Now then, Rachel," she said, as they all climbed out of the car, "would you and Kirsty like to go shopping on your own? I have some presents to buy which I don't want you to see!"

"Like what?" Rachel asked curiously.

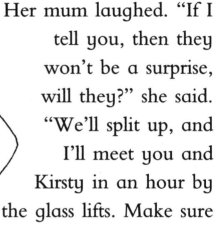 Her mum laughed. "If I tell you, then they won't be a surprise, will they?" she said. "We'll split up, and I'll meet you and Kirsty in an hour by the glass lifts. Make sure you stay inside the shopping centre."

"OK," the girls agreed.

Mrs Walker went to get the lift, while the girls stayed on the ground floor. They walked through the shopping centre, looking at the Christmas displays in the shop windows and chatting happily.

Christmas songs were playing over the speaker system, and people were bustling to and fro carrying lots of shopping bags.

Rachel and Kirsty had soon bought the few presents they had left to get. Kirsty bought some pretty silver earrings for her mum, and Rachel bought a diary for her dad.

"Are you OK in there, Holly?" Kirsty whispered, putting the earrings into her other pocket.

Holly nodded. She was peeping out from Kirsty's pocket to see what was going on. But she was so small, nobody noticed her amongst the hustle and bustle.

"Come and see the Christmas display," Rachel said to Kirsty. "It's beautiful."

Kirsty nodded eagerly, and Rachel led the way to the big central square of the shopping centre. There, right in front of them, was Santa's Grotto.

"Wow!" said Kirsty, her eyes wide. "This is fantastic!"

The grotto was a huge white tent
covered in sparkling lights that changed
colour from white to blue to
silver and then back
again. Long, glittering
icicles hung from the
roof. The tent was
surrounded by
fake snow, and
there were life-size
toy polar bears
and penguins that
waved at the
shoppers going by.
Near the tent was a
small ice rink. Boys and girls
dressed as elves were skating to and fro,
some carrying brightly-wrapped parcels,
others performing acrobatics and tumbles.

A pretty little bridge made of sparkling icicles led the way into the grotto.

"Isn't it lovely?" Rachel said, as they moved closer to get a better look.

There was a long queue of children waiting to see Santa. Rachel and Kirsty were standing near the bridge, watching the elves on the ice rink, when a little girl ran out of the grotto to join her mum. She seemed upset and Kirsty and Rachel couldn't help overhearing what she said.

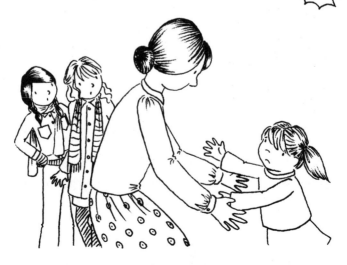

"Did you have a good time, darling?" the mother asked.

"Well, Santa's sleigh was all bright and sparkly," the little girl told her breathlessly, "and his reindeer were furry and friendly. But Santa wasn't very nice!" She stuck her bottom lip out as if she was about to cry. "He wouldn't let me have a present, even though he had lots and lots. And he was all cold and spiky!"

Immediately Rachel's ears pricked up. That didn't sound like Santa at all. But it did sound like someone else she knew — someone mean and tricky and cunning. Rachel thought they might just have found Jack Frost!

Not the Real Santa!

"Kirsty!" Rachel said, pulling her friend to one side so their conversation wouldn't be overheard. "Did you and Holly hear that? I think Jack Frost might be inside the grotto, pretending to be Santa!"

Kirsty stared at Rachel. "You could be right!" she gasped.

"Yes," Holly piped up. "We'd better check it out."

"How are we going to get into the tent?" asked Rachel. "It'll take ages if we have to queue."

"She's right," Kirsty said. "Let's try and slip in round the back and see what's going on."

The girls crept round the back of the grotto, keeping a sharp eye out for anyone who might try to stop them. But they found the tent was tied down so firmly, they couldn't sneak underneath.

"Leave this to me!" Holly whispered. She waved her wand, and a shower of sparkling red fairy dust fell onto a corner of the tent. Immediately the ropes loosened, and that part of the canvas curled upwards.

"Thanks, Holly!" said Rachel. "Come on, Kirsty."

The two girls crept cautiously under the edge of the tent and into the grotto. Inside were lots of glittering ice-covered rocks. Rachel, Kirsty and Holly hid behind them while they looked around.

The grotto was lit with magical, rainbow-coloured lanterns which glowed in the dim interior. Long, gleaming icicles hung from the ceiling, and a big Christmas tree stood in one corner, decorated with shiny silver baubles and multi-coloured fairy lights.

Kirsty shivered. The air inside the tent felt cold and frosty. "It's really chilly in here," she whispered. "Jack Frost must be nearby."

And sure enough, there, in the middle
of the room was Santa's beautiful
sparkling sleigh, complete with hundreds
of presents, eight magic reindeer and
Jack Frost! He was ripping open a
parcel, although the ground in front of
him was already littered with discarded
wrapping paper. He wore a red Santa
suit and a big fake white beard. But he
still looked his mean, cold spiky self.

"Bring me another!" he roared, tossing
aside the game of Snakes and Ladders
he'd just opened.

His goblin servants came rushing from
every corner of the grotto. They were all
carrying parcels, which they pushed into
Jack Frost's greedy hands. Rachel and
Kirsty held their breath nervously as
goblins hurried past their hiding place.

Suddenly Kirsty spotted
something. "Look!"
she hissed, pointing
at the sleigh. "It's
one of the special
presents!" The
gold-wrapped
parcel was sitting at
the back of the sleigh,
on top of a pile of other toys.

"You're right," Holly whispered
excitedly. "And the third one must still
be on the sleigh somewhere, too. It
doesn't look as though Jack Frost has
already opened it."

"But however are we going to get
hold of them without Jack Frost and his
goblins spotting us?" Rachel asked
anxiously.

"If we keep behind the rocks, we can crawl round to the back of the sleigh without being seen," said Kirsty.

"And I can help you," Holly added eagerly. "I'll distract Jack Frost and the goblins."

"What are you going to do?" asked Kirsty

"I'll magic myself inside one of the presents that Jack Frost is opening," Holly replied. "That'll give him a shock!"

"That's a great idea," Rachel declared. "Now, we'll creep up to the back of the sleigh. Then, while Holly creates a diversion, you grab the present, Kirsty, and I'll try to drop the magic crown on Jack Frost's head."

"OK. Let's go," Kirsty whispered.

Holly nodded. She waved her wand above her head and immediately disappeared.

Rachel and Kirsty began to crawl on their hands and knees towards the sleigh, keeping out of sight behind the rocks. Jack Frost was far too busy unwrapping presents to notice them.

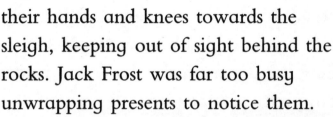

And, luckily, the goblins were preoccupied with running backwards and forwards, trying to keep their grumpy master happy.

Their hearts thumping, the girls drew nearer to the sleigh. The special present was so close now that Kirsty could reach out and touch it.

"Now we just wait for Holly to make her move," Rachel whispered.

The girls watched Jack Frost ripping the paper off yet another parcel. "I'm bored," he grumbled coldly. "Why can't I get a really nice present?" He threw the paper on the floor, and held up a pretty wooden box. "I wonder what's in here?" he muttered.

Suddenly the lid of the
box burst open. Holly
shot out in a huge
shower of glittering
red holly berries
and fairy dust,
making Jack Frost
and the goblins
cough and splutter.

"This is our chance!" Kirsty said to
Rachel, as Jack Frost and his goblins
stared at Holly in stunned surprise.

Rachel nodded and together the girls
moved towards Jack Frost.

The Chase is on...

Kirsty stretched out her hand for the special parcel. Meanwhile, Rachel pulled the crown out of her pocket, and stood up, ready to drop it onto the fake Santa's head.

"What's going on?" Jack Frost shouted, still rubbing fairy dust out of his eyes. "It's that pesky Christmas Fairy, isn't it? Grab her!"

Kirsty had her hands on the parcel now, and Rachel was leaning over the sleigh with the crown. But just then, one of the goblins spotted her. "Look out!" he screeched, pointing a bony finger at Rachel.

Jack Frost spun round. His cold, hard eyes met Rachel's and she felt herself shiver. Quickly, Jack Frost waved his wand, and immediately the reindeer galloped off, pulling the sleigh behind them. Luckily, Kirsty was still hanging onto the ribbon of the parcel.

As the sleigh moved away, the present tumbled off the back and fell safely into her arms.

"I want you to grab that fairy!" Jack Frost roared at his goblin servants as the reindeer galloped towards the tent entrance, taking the sleigh with them. "And those interfering girls, too!"

"Kirsty! Rachel!" shouted Holly, who was zooming up and away from the goblins. "You've got to get out of here!"

The reindeer galloped out of the tent and flew up into the air above the shoppers. As the sleigh soared overhead, the shoppers looked up in amazement. They gasped, and then began clapping and cheering, thinking it was some sort of fabulous Christmas magic show.

The sleigh flew through the shopping centre and out of the big double doors. Meanwhile, the goblins were closing in on the girls, backing them into a corner of the tent. "We've got you now!" one of them snarled.

"You can't get the better of us!" boasted another.

Kirsty and Rachel felt very scared. "Split up and run for it, when I give the word!" Rachel whispered. She waited until the goblins were quite close, and then shouted, "Now!"

Immediately, she and Kirsty ran as fast as they could in opposite directions. The goblins chased after them, but there was a lot of pushing and shoving and shouting as the clumsy goblins bumped into each other and tripped over their own feet.

In the middle of the chaos, Rachel and Kirsty both headed for the doorway. Kirsty reached it first. She noticed that Rachel was nearly at the exit, too, but a goblin was very close behind her, and as Kirsty slipped out of the tent, she saw the goblin make a grab for her friend!

The Great Escape

The goblin missed Rachel and fell over, tripping up another goblin who was hot on his heels. The girls had escaped from the grotto, but they knew that the goblins were right behind them. They had hardly any time to get away.

"Quick, Kirsty!" Rachel shouted. "Those support ropes at the back of the tent — we need to pull them out!"

Kirsty knew exactly what Rachel had in mind. The two girls began pulling and heaving at the ropes with all their might.

Suddenly there was a creaking sound and the ropes gave way. The large white tent wobbled a little and then fell to the ground, trapping the goblins underneath the heavy white canvas.

"We did it!" Kirsty gasped. "Well done, Rachel. That was a brilliant idea!"

"Yes, but I think we'd better get out of here before those goblins escape," Rachel whispered. "It's almost time to meet Mum anyway."

"Where's Holly?" asked Kirsty, looking around.

"Here I am!" called a tiny, silvery voice, and Holly zoomed over to land on Kirsty's shoulder. All the shoppers were too busy staring at the collapsed tent to notice the tiny fairy.

"Are you all right?" Rachel asked anxiously.

"I'm fine," Holly beamed. "Thank you for getting the second present. The Fairy King and Queen will be pleased!"

Kirsty held the parcel out and Holly waved her wand over it. Fairy dust fluttered down around it and the present promptly vanished back to Fairyland.

"I almost got the crown on Jack Frost's head!" Rachel sighed, as she pused it carefully back into her pocket. "But he got away again. And we don't know where he's gone."

"Oh, yes, we do!" Holly told her excitedly. "While you were escaping from the goblins, I followed the sleigh and spoke to one of my reindeer friends."

"What did he say?" asked Rachel eagerly.

"He told me Jack Frost is really annoyed that we keep finding him in the human world," Holly explained.

"He wants to open all of Santa's presents in peace and quiet. So he's told the reindeer to take him to his ice castle right away."

"His ice castle!" Kirsty exclaimed. "Is that where Jack Frost lives?"

Holly nodded.

"Do you know where it is, Holly?" Rachel asked.

"Yes," Holly replied. "It's a cold, scary place, but I can take you there tomorrow, if you still want to help?"

"Of course we do!" said Kirsty and Rachel together.

Holly beamed at them. "Then I'll
whizz back to Fairyland now and
report to the King and Queen,"
she went on. "Can you
get me out of this
shopping centre?"

"Of course," Kirsty
said smiling. While
Holly hid under Kirsty's
scarf, the girls walked quickly over to
one of the doors that led out into the
car park. When nobody was looking,
Holly slipped out from under the scarf,

gave the girls a cheery
wave and then zoomed
up into the sky. The
girls watched her
fly away until she
was out of sight.

Then they hurried back through the shopping centre towards the glass lifts, where they had promised to meet Rachel's mum.

Mrs Walker was already waiting for them, holding lots of exciting-looking carrier bags. "Hello, girls," she smiled. "I thought you'd got lost! Did you get everything you wanted?" "Almost!" Rachel replied, with a quick glance at Kirsty.

"Well, did you see Santa's grotto?"
Mrs Walker went on, leading the way
back to the car. "I heard it was very
beautiful – until it collapsed! But some
of the parents were complaining that
Father Christmas was rather grumpy."

Rachel and Kirsty
grinned at each
other. "He was!"
Kirsty agreed.

"I wonder
what's going
to happen
tomorrow,
Rachel," Kirsty
whispered as Mrs
Walker unlocked the car.

"Jack Frost's ice castle sounds scary."

"I know," Rachel whispered back.

"But we can't let our fairy friends down."

"No," Kirsty agreed firmly. "We have to get Santa's sleigh and the third present."

"And this time we'll get that magic crown on Jack Frost's head!" added Rachel. The girls exchanged a determined smile and climbed into the car, feeling very excited and a little bit nervous about just what tomorrow might have in store!

The Night Before Christmas

Contents

Winter Wonderland   119

The Ice Castle   125

Capture!   137

A Magical Journey   149

A Fairy Merry Christmas   159

Winter Wonderland

Rachel opened her eyes and yawned. She sat up in bed and looked across at Kirsty, who was still asleep. "It's Christmas Eve!" Rachel said to herself excitedly. But it would only be a merry Christmas if they managed to get Santa's sleigh and all the presents back to Santa today.

If they didn't, greedy Jack Frost would spoil everything.

Rachel pushed back the duvet and shivered. Even though the central heating was on, there was still a chill in the air. She went across to the window and looked outside. "Oh!" she gasped.

It had snowed heavily during the night, and the trees, the lawn and the flowerbeds were all hidden under a thick blanket of sparkling white snow.

"What is it?" Kirsty yawned.

"Sorry, did I wake you?" asked Rachel. "I was just so surprised to see the snow."

"Snow!" Kirsty gasped. She jumped out of bed and ran over to join Rachel. They both peered out of the frosty window.

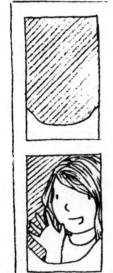

"It looks like we're going to have a white Christmas," Rachel smiled.

"It'll be the best Christmas ever," Kirsty agreed. "As long as we make it back from Jack Frost's ice castle…"

"Are you scared?" asked Rachel.

"A bit," Kirsty replied. "But I'm not giving up. Are you?"

"No way!" Rachel laughed. "Come on. Let's get dressed and have breakfast. Then we can go outside."

The two girls hurried downstairs for scrambled eggs and toast. Then they pulled on their coats and boots, and ran out into the garden. Their feet sank into the soft snow, leaving tracks all over the lawn. It started snowing again, and pretty snowflakes drifted down around them.

Kirsty rolled a snowball in her hands.
"Let's have a snowball
fight!" she grinned, and
threw it at Rachel.

Laughing, Rachel
ducked, but before the
snowball reached her, it
exploded in the air like a
firework. Tiny sparkling icicles of red
fire shot in all directions. As Kirsty and
Rachel watched in amazement, Holly
burst out of the snowball.

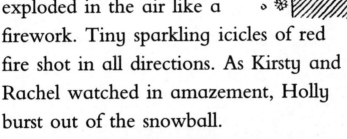

"Here I am!" she cried, shaking
snowflakes from her red dress. " Are
you ready, girls? It's time to go to Jack
Frost's ice castle!"

The Ice Castle

"We're ready!" Rachel said bravely.

Kirsty nodded and checked her pocket to make sure she had the magic crown.

Then Holly waved her wand in the air. Berry-red fairy dust drifted down over the girls, and they began to shrink. In a moment, they were fairy-sized with thin, gauzy wings on their backs.

Holly fluttered up into the air, and Rachel and Kirsty followed her.

"Here we go, then!" Holly said, waving her wand again.

It was snowing quite heavily now, and the falling snowflakes began to spin and dance around the girls until Rachel and Kirsty couldn't see anything at all.

Then, the blizzard of snow cleared as quickly as it had begun. Rachel and Kirsty gasped. They were no longer in the Walkers' back garden.
Instead, they were standing in a tree, staring up at Jack Frost's ice castle.

The castle stood on a tall hill, under a gloomy, grey winter sky. It was built from sheets of ice, and it had four towers tipped with icy blue turrets. The ice glittered and gleamed like diamonds, but the palace still looked cold and scary.

"Be careful," Holly whispered, as a couple of goblins wandered underneath the tree. "There are goblins everywhere. We'll never get in through the main gate."

"Maybe we can find a way in from the battlements," Rachel suggested, looking upwards.

"Good idea," Holly replied. "Follow me." The girls followed Holly as she flew up towards one of the ice-blue turrets. "See what I mean?" Holly said quietly. Rachel and Holly peered down at the castle beneath them.

Holly was right. There were goblin guards on every door.

"Maybe we can find an open window," whispered Rachel.

Holly nodded. "Let's split up and take a look. We'll meet back here in a few minutes."

They flew off in different directions. Kirsty went to look around the tops of the towers, one by one. There were lots of windows, but all of them were locked. She flew back to meet Rachel and Holly.

Rachel was already waiting. "I didn't have any luck," she sighed. "Did you?"

Kirsty shook her head sadly.

At that moment, Holly fluttered down to join them.

"You were a long time," said Kirsty.

"I had to hide from one of the goblins," Holly explained. "He was marching along the battlements on guard duty."

"We didn't find any open windows," Rachel told her. "Did you?"

Holly shook her head. "No, but I found another way in!" she grinned. "Follow me!"

Holly led the girls to a place on the battlements and pointed at the icy floor. "Look!" she said.

"A trapdoor!" Kirsty gasped.

Holly nodded. "When I was hiding from the goblin, I saw him lift the trapdoor and go into the castle," she told them. "And I don't think he bolted it on the other side."

131

They checked that there were no goblins around, and then flew down to the trapdoor. It was a slab of ice with a steel ring in the top.

"It looks very heavy," Rachel said with a frown.

"That's no problem," Holly said smiling. She waved her wand and the trapdoor suddenly flew open in a whirl of fairy dust.

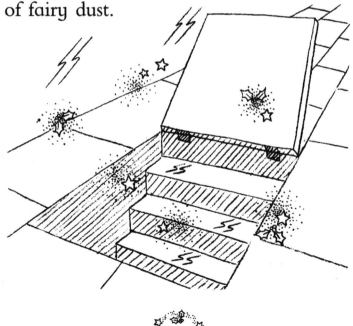

Below were steps of ice, leading down into the castle. Shivering with cold, Rachel, Kirsty and Holly flew inside.

"We must start looking for Santa's sleigh right away," Holly whispered to the girls.

"It's not easy to hide a sleigh and eight reindeer!" said Rachel thoughtfully.

"Maybe they're in the stables?" Kirsty suggested.

"That's a good place to start," said Holly. "But keep a sharp look-out for goblins!"

The friends flew down the winding staircase towards the ground floor of the castle. But as they fluttered round a corner of the stairs, they bumped straight into a goblin who was on his way up.

"Fairies!" roared the goblin furiously. "What are you doing here?" He grabbed at Holly, but missed as she darted out of reach. "Help! Fairies!"

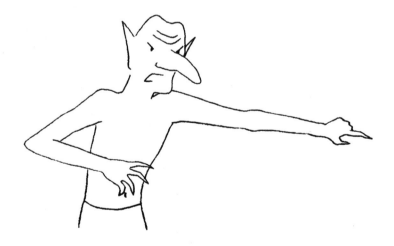

Holly, Rachel and Kirsty turned and whizzed back up the stairs. But as they reached the next corner, they heard the loud clatter of footsteps. Six more goblins rushed towards them!

Capture!

The friends tried to dodge out of the way, but they were completely surrounded by goblins. Holly and Rachel were grabbed immediately. Kirsty tried to fly away overhead, but one goblin jumped onto another's shoulders and caught hold of her ankle.

The goblins laughed gleefully.

"Now you're our prisoners!" they gloated. "Jack Frost is going to be very pleased with us!"

The goblins took the friends through the ice castle and into the Great Hall. It was a huge room carved from shining sheets of ice. At one end was Jack Frost's throne. It looked very grand, made out of glittering icicles that had been twisted into shape.

But Jack Frost wasn't sitting on his throne. He was in Santa's sleigh! The reindeer were still harnessed to it, and they were feeding on bales of hay. Jack Frost was unwrapping more presents, and the floor was covered with wrapping paper and ribbons.

Rachel, Holly and Kirsty trembled as the goblins pushed them towards Jack Frost.

"Look what we've brought you!" one of the goblins called triumphantly.

Jack Frost looked up at the girls. "You again!" he snarled, staring at them with cold, hard eyes. "You're always trying to spoil my fun!"

He shook his fist, and Rachel gasped

as she saw the present Jack Frost was holding in his other hand. He hadn't opened it yet. It was still wrapped in its pretty gold paper, and tied with a bow of rainbow colours. It was the third special present that the King and Queen of the fairies had asked the girls to find!

Rachel glanced at Kirsty and Holly.
She could see that they'd spotted the
present too. But how were they going
to stop Jack Frost from opening it?

Kirsty was thinking the same thing as
Rachel. She stared down at
the piles of wrapping
paper on the floor,
and suddenly an
idea struck her.

"What am
I going to do
with you?" Jack
Frost was muttering,
tapping his long, thin
fingers on top of the
present. "I think I'll put you in my
deepest ice dungeon, and leave you
there for one hundred years!"

"Rachel," Kirsty whispered. "I've got an idea. Can you distract the goblins and Jack Frost for a few moments?"

Rachel looked at her friend curiously, then nodded. "OK," she whispered back.

"Shall we take them to the dungeons, master?" asked one of the goblins.

"I haven't decided yet," Jack Frost snapped. "Now be quiet while I open this present." He lifted the parcel and shook it. "I can't wait to see what's inside!"

The goblins pressed forward, eager to see what was inside the parcel too. The goblin who was holding Rachel loosened his grip slightly, and Rachel saw her chance. She zoomed up into the air, then flew straight for the door.

"Seize her!" Jack Frost yelled furiously.

The goblins rushed after Rachel, shouting instructions and tripping over each other's feet.

Meanwhile, Kirsty bent down and grabbed a piece of silver wrapping paper and a purple ribbon from the floor. While Jack Frost was watching the goblins, Kirsty pulled the gold bag with the magic crown in it out of her pocket and quickly wrapped it in the silver paper. Then she tied the ribbon around the parcel. Holly gave her a puzzled look. She had no idea what Kirsty was up to!

Jack Frost was getting more and more angry as his goblins failed to catch Rachel. Eventually, he waved his wand, and instantly Rachel's wings froze in mid-air. She fell to the ground, landing on top of two goblins.

"Now!" Jack Frost snapped, as two more goblins dragged Rachel to her feet. "I'm going to open this present!"

"Please, Your Majesty," said Kirsty, stepping forward. "May I say something?"

Jack Frost glared at her. "Make it quick!" he said crossly.

"Won't you take pity on us?" asked Kirsty. "We only came here to get this one very special present." And she held up the crown, wrapped in silver paper. "It's for the Fairy King, you see, and it's very important. Won't you let us take it to him?"

Jack Frost's beady eyes lit up as he stared at the parcel Kirsty was holding. "A present for King Oberon?" he muttered. "Give it to me!"

"But—" Kirsty began.

"Now!" Jack Frost roared.

A goblin pushed Kirsty forward. Jack

Frost dropped the present he was holding, and snatched the other from Kirsty's hands.

Kirsty tried not to smile. She knew greedy Jack Frost wouldn't be able to resist taking the Fairy King's present for himself! Now he was ripping the ribbon and paper away to reveal the golden bag. He put his hand inside and drew out the glittering crown.

"Aha!" he declared triumphantly. "It's a new crown! Well, I'll have that!" He lifted the crown and lowered it onto his frosty white hair.

Immediately, Jack Frost vanished!

A Magical Journey

The goblins gasped in surprise and fear.
They didn't know what had happened
to their master, and they thought they
might be next! They ran around the
Great Hall in panic. Some tried to hide
under the piles of wrapping paper,
while others huddled behind giant
icicles.

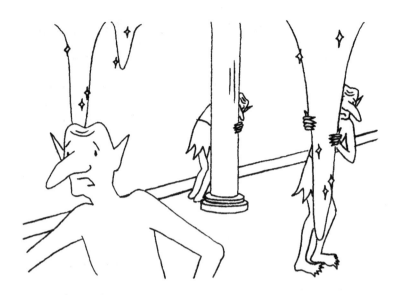

"Well done, Kirsty!" Holly laughed.

"Jack Frost's been sent straight to the Fairy King and Queen," cried Rachel in delight. She jumped into the magic sleigh and picked up the third present. "And it's time we were leaving, too!"

"But how are we going to get out of the castle?" asked Kirsty, as she hopped on board.

"Don't worry about that," Holly said cheerfully. "The sleigh's magic, you know!" She patted one of the reindeer on the head. "Take us back to Santa, please, my friends!"

The reindeer tossed their antlers joyfully, and began to gallop off down the Great Hall. Goblins jumped out of the way as the sleigh picked up speed. Then it rose into the air, heading for the icy roof.

"Oh!" gasped Rachel. "We're going to crash!"

But, magically, the ice melted away as the sleigh approached, and soon the girls were soaring out of the castle, and up into the clouds. Then the reindeer raced across the sky so fast, that everything was a blur as the wind rushed past the sleigh.

"Here's Santa's workshop!" Holly called at last.

The reindeer had slowed, and the sleigh was floating towards the ground. Rachel and Kirsty peered out eagerly.

Below them, they saw the pretty log
cabin which they had seen in the fairy
pool. And there was a large crowd of
elves outside, dancing in the snow, the
bells on their hats tinkling merrily.

"Hurrah!" they cried happily.
"You've found the sleigh and the
reindeer!" As the sleigh
landed, the elves ran
over to pet the
reindeer and feed
them carrots.

Rachel and Kirsty
gasped with delight
as Santa himself
came dashing out of
the cabin. He was in
such a hurry he hadn't
even buttoned up his red coat.

"Welcome! Welcome!" Santa called, beaming all over his jolly face. "My beautiful sleigh and my precious reindeer are safe, thanks to you!"

"Are we in time to save Christmas, Santa?" Rachel asked anxiously.

Santa nodded. "Oh, yes," he smiled. "It's going to be a wonderful Christmas!"

"But what about the presents Jack Frost opened?" Kirsty wanted to know. "Does that mean some children won't get anything?"

"Oh, no!" Santa boomed, looking quite shocked. "That would never do! My elves have made plenty of extra presents."

As he spoke, a group of elves ran out of the cabin, carrying armfuls of brightly-coloured gifts which they piled up in the magic sleigh.

"Now," said Santa, when the sleigh was full of presents once again. "The King and Queen will be wanting to see you.

Come with me and I'll drop you off on my way to deliver these gifts."

Rachel and Kirsty climbed back into the sleigh looking thrilled. They were going to ride with Santa Claus on Christmas Eve!

Holly joined them, as Santa picked up the reins. "Let's go, my friends!" Santa called happily to the reindeer. "We have a lot of work to do today!"

Rachel and Kirsty grinned at each other as the sleigh rose up into the sky again, and set off for Fairyland.

A Fairy Merry Christmas

As Santa's sleigh drew closer to Fairyland, the girls and Holly could see sparkling fireworks exploding below them. Sweet music, and the sound of fairy laughter drifted up to the sleigh.

"There's a big party at the palace," Holly smiled. "They've heard the good news."

The reindeer swooped lower, and
there was a shout of welcome from the
fairies below as they spotted the sleigh.
Rachel and Kirsty waved as they saw
all their old friends waiting for them.

"Well done!" called King Oberon
as the sleigh landed. "

You've helped Holly save Christmas!" Queen Titania added.

The fairies cheered as Rachel, Kirsty and Holly stepped out of the sleigh.

"We brought you this," Rachel said, handing the third special present to the King.

"Thank you!" the King beamed. "Won't you stay and join the party, Santa?"

Santa shook his head. "I'd love to, but I have a lot of work to do!" he laughed. He shook the reins. "Merry Christmas!"

"Merry Christmas!" everyone called, as the silver sleigh flew out of sight.

"What's happened to Jack Frost?" asked Rachel.

The King looked stern. "He has had his magic powers taken away from him," he explained.

"And he must stay in his ice castle for a whole year before he is allowed to use magic again!" the Queen said. "But now it's time to celebrate Christmas, and we have special gifts for all three of you."

She clapped her hands, and two small fairies hurried forward. They carried the two special presents which Holly had brought back to Fairyland earlier.

"These presents are particularly special because they are for the three of you!" the Queen said.

Rachel, Holly and Kirsty gasped in surprise, and everyone laughed.

"Since it's Christmas Eve, you can open them right away," smiled the King. And he handed Holly the parcel that Rachel had just given him.

Eagerly Holly tore the gold paper off the parcel, and peeped inside the box.

"A new wand!" she breathed. "It's beautiful!"

"It is extra sparkly and powerful," Queen Titania told her, as Holly twirled the wand above her head. It left a trail of magic sparkles behind it, and made the sweet sound of tinkling Christmas bells. "It will help you make Christmas more magical than ever before," the Queen smiled.

"Thank you!" Holly beamed.

The Queen handed the other two presents to Rachel and Kirsty. They couldn't wait to see what was inside! Rachel managed to open hers a second before Kirsty, and she gasped with delight.

"It's a fairy doll!" Rachel said, her eyes shining. "Look, Kirsty – a fairy for the top of the Christmas tree!"

The doll sparkled and shone with magic. She wore a white dress which glittered with silver and gold, and a sparkling crown on her long hair. Kirsty had one exactly the same.

"I can't wait to get home and put it on our Christmas tree!" Kirsty said, smiling happily.

"There's just one more thing," the Queen laughed. "These dolls are magic. Every year they will bring you a special Christmas present from the fairies!"

Rachel and Kirsty were thrilled to bits. They'd never expected this!

"But we mustn't keep you any longer," the King said suddenly. "It's time for you to go home, or you'll be late for Christmas!"

Quickly the girls said their goodbyes. They both had a special hug for Holly,

and then the Queen
waved her wand.
"Thank you!"
she called.
"And Merry
Christmas!"
  "Merry
Christmas!"
Rachel and
Kirsty replied, as
they were caught up in
a whirl of magic fairy dust.

"Merry Christmas!" called all the
fairies.

Suddenly the silvery fairy voices died
away, the magic dust cleared, and
Rachel and Kirsty found themselves
back to their normal size in the
Walkers' garden.

"We did it, Rachel!" Kirsty laughed breathlessly. "We saved Christmas!"

"Let's go inside and put my fairy doll on the Christmas tree," Rachel grinned.

The girls ran inside. Kirsty watched as Rachel fixed the fairy doll carefully to the top of the tree.

"She looks lovely!" Rachel said happily.

Just then the doorbell rang. Rachel
ran to see who it was,
and found Kirsty's
mum and dad
standing outside.

"Merry
Christmas!"
said Mr and
Mrs Tate with
a smile.

"Mum! Dad!"
Kirsty cried,
rushing over to them.

Mr and Mrs Tate stayed for tea and
mince pies, and then it was time for
Kirsty to leave. She gave Buttons a
cuddle, and Rachel a hug.

"Have a great Christmas!" Kirsty told
her friend.

"You too," Rachel replied. Then she stood on the doorstep with her mum and dad, waving at the Tates as they drove away.

Mr and Mrs Walker closed the front door and returned to the cosy living-room, but Rachel stayed in the hall for a moment with Buttons. She stared up at the glittering fairy on top of the tree.

Then Rachel blinked hard. Was she seeing things? The fairy had smiled at her. And a cloud of magic sparkles had drifted from her wand!

Rachel looked down to
see where the sparkles
had fallen – and
there was a
present under the
tree that hadn't
been there before.
It was wrapped in
gold paper and tied
with a bow that
glittered in all the
colours of the rainbow.

Rachel smiled and patted Buttons.
This really was going to be the best
Christmas ever!

Win a Rainbow Magic
Sparkly T-Shirt and Goody Bag!

There are 9 magic holly leaves in Holly the Christmas
Fairy and each one has a secret letter in it. Find all
nine letters and re-arrange them to make a special
Fairyland word, then send it to us. Each month we will
put the entries into a draw. The winner will receive a
Rainbow Magic Sparkly T-shirt and Goody Bag!

Send your entry on a postcard to Rainbow Magic
Competition, Orchard Books, 96 Leonard Street,
London EC2A 4XD. Australian readers should write
to 32/45-51 Huntley Street, Alexandria, NSW 2015.
Don't forget to include your name and address.
Only one entry per child.

FERN THE GREEN FAIRY
1-84362-019-7

SAFFRON THE YELLOW FAIRY
1-84362-018-9

AMBER THE ORANGE FAIRY
1-84362-017-0

RUBY THE RED FAIRY
1-84362-016-2

HEATHER THE VIOLET FAIRY
1-84362-022-7

IZZY THE INDIGO FAIRY
1-84362-021-9

SKY THE BLUE FAIRY
1-84362-020-0

RAINBOW magic

The Weather Fairies

CRYSTAL THE SNOW FAIRY
1-84362-633-0

ABIGAIL THE BREEZE FAIRY
1-84362-634-9

PEARL THE CLOUD FAIRY
1-84362-635-7

GOLDIE THE SUNSHINE FAIRY
1-84362-641-1

EVIE THE MIST FAIRY
1-84362-636-5

STORM THE LIGHTNING FAIRY
1-84362-637-3

HAYLEY THE RAIN FAIRY
1-84362-638-1

Collect all of the Rainbow Magic books!

by Daisy Meadows

Ruby the Red Fairy	ISBN	1 84362 016 2
Amber the Orange Fairy	ISBN	1 84362 017 0
Saffron the Yellow Fairy	ISBN	1 84362 018 9
Fern the Green Fairy	ISBN	1 84362 019 7
Sky the Blue Fairy	ISBN	1 84362 020 0
Izzy the Indigo Fairy	ISBN	1 84362 021 9
Heather the Violet Fairy	ISBN	1 84362 022 7

The Weather Fairies

Crystal the Snow Fairy	ISBN	1 84362 633 0
Abigail the Breeze Fairy	ISBN	1 84362 634 9
Pearl the Cloud Fairy	ISBN	1 84362 635 7
Goldie the Sunshine Fairy	ISBN	1 84362 641 1
Evie the Mist Fairy	ISBN	1 84362 636 5
Storm the Lightning Fairy	ISBN	1 84362 637 3
Hayley the Rain Fairy	ISBN	1 84362 638 1

| Holly the Christmas Fairy | ISBN | 1 84362 661 6 |

All priced at £3.99
Rainbow Magic books are available from all good bookshops,
or can be ordered direct from the publisher:
Orchard Books, PO BOX 29, Douglas IM99 1BQ
Credit card orders please telephone 01624 836000
or fax 01624 837033 or visit our Internet site: www.wattspub.co.uk
or e-mail: bookshop@enterprise.net for details.

To order please quote title, author and ISBN
and your full name and address.
Cheques and postal orders should be made payable to 'Bookpost plc.'
Postage and packing is FREE within the UK
(overseas customers should add £1.00 per book).

Prices and availability are subject to change.